TWIST ◆ PLOT

GOLDEN SWORD OF DRAGONWALK

R.L. STINE

INTERIOR ILLUSTRATIONS BY DAVID FEBLAND

AN
APPLE
PAPERBACK

SCHOLASTIC INC.
New York Toronto London Auckland Sydney

LOOK FOR THESE TWISTAPLOT® BOOKS
BY R.L. STINE:

Horrors of the Haunted Museum

The Time Raider

ISBN 0-590-48557-1

12 11 10 9 8 7 6 5 4 3   5 6 7 8 9/9 0/0

Printed in the U.S.A.   40

BEWARE!!!

DO NOT READ
THIS BOOK
FROM
BEGINNING TO END

You are about to enter the medieval kingdom of Dragonwalk. It takes courage to visit this once-proud land, for the people who lived here have all been driven out. Today, Dragonwalk is populated by sorcerers of dark forces, dragons who live only to destroy, and nightmare creatures who feed on evil and kill for pleasure.

Knights of the Round Table travel around the borders of Dragonwalk rather than risk the terrors that await within. Carrying the legendary Golden Sword of this kingdom, you venture forward with a mission — to rid Dragonwalk of the evil forces that have held it in darkness for so many centuries.

You will make your own decisions and choose your own paths by following the directions at the bottom of each page. If you choose well, the ancient honor scroll of heroes will include your name. If you take the wrong paths, the forces that have devoured Dragonwalk will devour you, too.

Fare well, traveler!

Now turn to PAGE 2.

2

A visit to Grandma Carmen's means a day of exploring, for your lonely, old grandmother lives in a tall mansion with hidden closets and passageways, and attic rooms that haven't been opened since long before you were born. You gobble down the toast and jam she has prepared for your lunch and ask to be excused. You can't wait to climb the cracked stairways and search out the fresh surprises the old house always offers.

"Just a moment, just a moment," Grandma Carmen says, wiping crumbs of toast from her chin with a yellowed lace napkin. "Before you disappear for the day, I have a little surprise for you."

The doorbell rings, and she walks down the long hallway to the front door. "There's the surprise now," she says. She opens the door, and a little girl walks in. It's Stacy, who lives down the street.

"What's the surprise?" you ask, impatient to begin your exploring.

"Stacy is the surprise," says Grandma Carmen. "I promised her mother you'd look after her this afternoon. You don't mind, do you?"

Go on to PAGE 3.

Don't mind?!? A seven-year-old girl underfoot while you have dark caverns to explore, mysterious passageways, and endless treasure-filled tunnels to travel?! Grandma Carmen looks at you sternly. "Of course I don't mind," you say quietly.

You climb the creaking attic stairs slowly, with Stacy right behind you. The two of you creep through dark rooms filled with wisps of cobwebs and dust thick as snow.

A curving passageway leads to another one, and at the end of this silent tunnel, a circular room unfolds, a room you have never seen before. "Now, don't touch anything unless I say it's okay," you tell Stacy.

But you are already too late. Stacy has picked up a large blue vase with strange writing around the base. "Isn't this pretty?" she asks, holding the vase up. As she does so, the bookcase on the far wall begins to slide open.

"Stacy — what have you done?" you cry, startled by the moving wall. "Look — a passageway behind the bookcase! A secret tunnel! Come on — let's see where it leads!"

"No," Stacy says, backing toward the doorway. "Let's get out of here! I'm scared!"

If you persuade Stacy to explore the secret passage with you, turn to PAGE 4.

If you don't want to argue and would rather try another room, turn to PAGE 6.

4

"Come on, Stacy, let's see what's on the other side," you plead. "I promise I'll take care of you, no matter what."

"And if it's something yucky we can leave right away?" she asks, starting to give in.

"I promise," you say, pulling her into the passageway. You hope it's the truth.

There is hazy sunshine on the other side of the passageway. You step out to find yourself at the edge of a silent forest. Peasants dressed in black, carrying sheaths of straw on their backs, walk slowly down a dirt path that leads to a dirty little town of straw huts in the distance.

"Welcome to Dragonwalk," a man's voice says quietly.

You turn around to find a bearded man in a black robe. There is no "welcome" in his eyes — just the same pain and unhappiness you have noticed in the eyes of the peasants who walk by in silence.

"You have not come at a happy time," the man says, as if he could read your thoughts. "Perhaps you have been chosen to rescue Dragonwalk from its plight."

"Who is he?" Stacy asks you.

"I am the sorcerer Merle," the man says.

"Don't you mean Merlin?" you ask.

"Are you kidding?! Merlin wouldn't be caught dead here! I am Merle, sorcerer of this dying kingdom."

Go on to PAGE 5.

"Dying?" you ask.

"Take me home," Stacy says.

"Dying because no one can get in or out of Dragonwalk. We are all held prisoner — to be fed to three starving dragons."

"Let's go. You promised!" Stacy cries.

"Wait a minute. Don't you want to have any fun?" you ask her.

"None of our knights has been able to defeat the dragons," Merle continues. "You have been sent here from another time and place. Perhaps you are the one who can free us from these three creatures and return happiness to Dragonwalk."

"Well, I'd like to help — " you begin.

"You promised! Let's get out of here now!" Stacy insists.

"There is one of the dragons — the biggest one," Merle says, pointing a trembling finger toward the forest.

You turn and see that the passageway leading back to Grandma Carmen's house is still there. You must decide what to do now.

If you choose to return to the safety of your grandmother's house and visit Dragonwalk at another time, turn to PAGE 11.

If you choose to battle the dragons of Dragonwalk, turn to PAGE 8.

"Okay, Stacy. It's okay," you say soothingly. "We don't have to explore the passageway. We don't have to have any fun at all today. It's fine with me."

"It's too dark in there," she says. She has backed up nearly to the door.

"Okay, we'll go to another room," you say, following her. "I know where there are some great old clothes we can try on. We can—"

But before you finish your sentence, you hear loud noises coming from the secret passageway—footsteps, then a scream of pain. You stare in amazement as a knight in full armor, carrying a golden-bladed sword above his head, staggers out of the dark passageway and falls to the floor at your feet.

"Help!" the knight cries weakly. He attempts to pull himself up, but falls back again. "I am in need of help."

"Let's get outta here!" Stacy manages to cry, her face white with fright. "Please— let's go—now!"

"He's in trouble," you say. "We've got to help him! We can't just leave him here in the attic!"

If you choose to follow Stacy out of the room as fast as you can, turn to PAGE 10.

If you choose to stay and help this mysterious intruder in the attic, turn to PAGE 12.

8

"There is little time," Merle cries. "For when the biggest dragon approaches, the other two are close behind."

"But I—I can't—you mean—I—" Your fear has taken the words from your mouth.

"That dragon looks *mean*," Stacy says.

"Thanks, Stacy," you say sarcastically.

The sorcerer Merle holds a golden sword. "This is the legendary Golden Sword of Dragonwalk," he says. "You've heard of it?"

"No. I don't think so," you say quickly. The dragon roars. The gray sky turns scarlet. Birds shriek in terror.

Merle puts the Golden Sword in your hand. "Many brave knights have displayed their courage behind this golden weapon."

"Please—Merle—no speeches," you cry. "What's so special about this sword?"

"It gives its bearer the power to use it," Merle says.

"How about immortality?" you ask. "Does it make its owner invincible? Unable to lose a battle?"

"No," Merle says quietly. "The key to victory is the order in which you kill the dragons. If you battle them in the correct order, you will win. If you battle them in the wrong order, not even the Golden Sword will keep you from being devoured!"

"Yuck," Stacy says, encouragingly.

Go on to PAGE 9.

"Well—what's the correct order?" you cry. The biggest dragon approaches. Behind it, you can see the fierce head of a slightly smaller dragon.

Merle shrugs his shoulders. "Beats me," he says. He turns and runs for cover, pulling Stacy with him. The Golden Sword is gripped tightly in your hand.

You must choose in which order you are going to fight the dragons. Only one order is correct. If you choose incorrectly, your stay in the kingdom of Dragonwalk will be short and not sweet.

Choose an order. Hold the Golden Sword high. And don't forget to duck!

If you choose to fight the dragons in this order—big, middle, little — turn to *PAGE* 14.

If you choose big, little, middle—turn to *PAGE* 15.

If you choose middle, big, little—turn to *PAGE* 19.

If you choose middle, little, big—turn to *PAGE* 22.

If you choose little, middle, big—turn to *PAGE* 23.

If you choose little, big, middle—turn to *PAGE* 25.

10

The sword falls from the knight's hand with a heavy clang. The knight moans from the agony of his wounds.

"You're right, Stacy—let's get outta here!" you cry. You both race toward the doorway. You are surprised to find the door closed. You turn the knob, but the door does not open. You both push against it as hard as you can, but it feels as if some kind of force is pushing back from the other side.

The knight pulls himself up onto one knee. "It is Ravenhurst's magic," he whispers, pointing toward the door. "You cannot escape. Ravenhurst will not let you leave this room alive!"

"But—what—what can we do?" you cry. You struggle to sound brave for Stacy's sake.

"You have no choice now but to help me," the knight says, his voice growing even more feeble. "Ravenhurst has given you no choice."

"What can *we* do?" you ask.

To find out, turn to PAGE 12.

"Let's get outta here!" Stacy cries, as the dragon approaches, each footstep a thunderclap.

"I'm with you!" you shout.

The two of you race back toward the open passageway. You've never run so fast in your life. But the passageway doesn't come any closer. The faster you run, the farther away the passageway seems.

"This is some kind of trick!" you yell. "It's moving away at the same speed we run toward it!"

"It is a sign that you must stay and fight!" Merle cries. He is right behind you.

"It is a sign that you are meant to carry the Golden Sword!" Merle stretches his arm forward, and a glowing gold sword appears in his hand. "Perhaps you—and the Golden Sword—can defeat the dragons that hold us all captive."

You have no choice now. The passageway is but a dim shadow in the distance. The dragon roars and rumbles forward. The Golden Sword gleams in the sunlight. You know that in a moment you will be fighting for your life.

Turn back to PAGE 8.

"Who are you? Where do you come from?" you cry, struggling to help the knight.

"I come from a kingdom known as Dragonwalk," he says in a voice that grows fainter with each word. "My kingdom has been the domain of evil for many years. I stood up to that evil—for I came to be possessor of the Golden Sword. But now I am mortally wounded. I must pass on the Golden Sword—and with it, the hopes of the few good people remaining in Dragonwalk. I have no choice but to pass it on to you."

He shoves the golden-bladed sword at you. It is heavier than you expect, and you drop it with a *thud*.

"Hold the sword tightly," the knight says, the color fading from his already pale face. "And may it bring you better fortune than it did me. The sorcerer Ravenhurst will follow me here. You must not let him through the passageway. You must not let his evil into your world. Go—go! You must travel through the black tunnel to free Dragonwalk of its enemies!"

"But I can't!" you cry, struggling to lift up the heavy sword to return it to him. "I can't go off into some medieval kingdom and fight sorcerers! I'm supposed to stay and take care of Stacy. So I really—"

"It's no use," Stacy says quietly, fighting to hold back tears. "He's dead, I think."

Go on to PAGE 13.

The knight has died. His death spurs you to action. "Come on—into the tunnel!" you scream at Stacy. "He left his hopes with us. We cannot disappoint him!"

"But what if we're not back by suppertime?" Stacy cries, as you drag her into the dark passageway. "Grandma Carmen will get worried!"

You don't hear her words. Your only thought is to get through that dark, cold passageway and find out what awaits you on the other side. You run as fast as you can, with Stacy struggling to keep up. You fall and feel wet earth on your knees. You pick yourself up and keep running.

Light. Gray light. Is that the sky? You are definitely running on dirt now. The passageway ends, and you are standing in a gray evening world of low, barren hills and scraggly shrubs.

"Ho, there!" a voice calls. You and Stacy, struggling to catch your breath, look up to see three men approaching, dressed in peasant robes.

"Maybe they're coming to help us," Stacy says, almost pleading for it to be true.

"Maybe they are Ravenhurst's men," you say. "We must fight to keep them out of the passageway!"

If you choose to wait and listen to them, turn to PAGE 16.

If you choose to fight, turn to PAGE 18.

You raise the Golden Sword and step forward to meet the biggest dragon. It feels as if you are stepping into a furnace. The dragon's ruby eyes glare into yours as his serpentine head arches in a toothy sneer.

"There's one thing I forgot to tell you!" Merle calls.

"What's that?" you ask.

"Don't fight the biggest one first! Everyone who tries the biggest one first loses immediately!"

"I wish you had told me that just a little bit sooner," you say.

It's a shame he hadn't. For then, maybe your stay in Dragonwalk would have been more pleasant, and this wouldn't be

THE END

The dragon roars an unfriendly welcome. You raise the Golden Sword, but stagger back from the force of the dragon's breath.

"A shield! I need a shield!" you cry.

The biggest dragon lifts its head in a cry of victory before the battle has even begun. The air itself seems to melt, turning to molten lava from the beast's fierce breath.

"Here—use this as a shield!" It is Stacy, carrying a large, flat piece of tree bark.

"Stacy—get back!" you scream.

The dragon roars again, this time with such heat and force that both you and Stacy are blown into the air. You feel yourself flying through the hot, steamy air.

Bump. Another *bump.* You have landed on a hard floor. Where are you? After what seems like hours, you open your eyes.

What luck! You are back in Grandma Carmen's house, back in the room, safe on the other side of the passageway. The dragon has blown you back.

But wait! You have not only traveled back to where you started, but the force of the dragon's breath has also blown you backward in time. You remember nothing of your first terrifying visit to Dragonwalk. You and Stacy just discovered the passageway. Stacy doesn't want to go through. But you are eager to explore. Will you both return to Dragonwalk?

Turn to PAGE 6.

As the three men come nearer, you see that only one of them is armed—and he does not have his sword drawn. You hold the Golden Sword tightly in front of you but do not move to use it.

"The Golden Sword!" one of the men cries. "How did you come to possess it?"

"A dying knight gave it to me," you say. You see that the three men are in awe of the sword.

"Then you have come to rescue Dragonwalk from its foes," one of the men says. "You do not seem to be a powerful knight or clever sorcerer. What are your powers?"

"Powers?" you ask. "Well, I—uh—"

"And what of the little girl?" one of them asks. "How will her powers aid you in your battles?"

"Battles?" Your voice cracks at the word. "Well, I was just taking care of her for the afternoon, and I couldn't leave her behind, so—"

A rustling in the trees causes the men to huddle closer together. The wind grows cold and the gray sky turns charcoal.

"We have no time for conversation," one of the men says in a whisper. "Ravenhurst is near. His magic takes many forms, all of them evil. We must prepare quickly. We have come to help you," he says.

Go on to PAGE 17.

"Where do we go? What do we do?" you ask, suddenly realizing that you will be involved in a serious battle.

"I want to go home," Stacy says. "Take me home right now."

You look around. There is no house. No passageway. No trace of the neighborhood you left—only low, grassy hills leading to a dark forest of bent and twisted trees.

"Ravenhurst will find you soon enough," one of the men says with a frown, ignoring Stacy's repeated demands to go home. "It isn't safe for all of us to travel together. You must choose one of us to help you in your battle against Ravenhurst's evil."

The three men introduce themselves. There is Elkar, a knight-warrior; Chalidor, an apprentice sorcerer; and Bendux, the wealthiest man in Dragonwalk.

Bendux greets you by holding up a bag filled with gold coins. "I have found that evil can always be fended off with gold," he says. Elkar insists that a powerful sword is a bigger help than any gold. And Chalidor boasts that magic spells are more powerful than might or wealth.

You must choose which of these men you will bring along to aid you in your battle against Ravenhurst. Choose only one of them—the other two will then disappear into the forest.

Then turn to PAGE 20.

As the men approach, you can see that they have no intention of helping you. They draw long swords as they run toward you. "Well . . . " you say, drawing up as much courage as you possess, "they'll know they've been in a fight!"

You reach for the Golden Sword.

"Uh—Stacy—did you bring the sword?"

She stares at you, too frightened to speak.

"Oh, no! I left it back in the room!" you scream, realizing your blunder.

The three men rush right past you, gleeful smiles on their evil faces. They run into the tunnel and—a few seconds later—are in Grandma Carmen's house. "Another triumph for the forces of evil!" you hear one of them shout. "Look, men—the Golden Sword is ours!"

In a few days, Grandma Carmen's once-quiet neighborhood is overrun by evil. Dragons roam the sidewalks, chewing up the hedges and swallowing pedestrians whole. Sorcerers change babies into toads, while knights in dark armor plunder, rob, throw litter in the streets, and laugh about it all the while.

It's all your fault. But don't bother to aplogize. Just throw a nut to that squirrel over there. That squirrel is your grandmother after her run-in with an evil sorcerer!

THE END

Sure, you'd *rather* fight the middle one than the biggest one. But it's the biggest one that's walking in front.

You've chosen to fight the middle one first. But how are you going to get the biggest one out of the way so that you can get to the middle one?

A good question??

Well . . . let's not call you dumb. Let's just call you . . . Dragon Meat!

THE END

"Ravenhurst is over three hundred years old," your new traveling companion tells you. "In that time, many have owned the Golden Sword. Many have fought to rid Dragonwalk of his evil. And all have failed."

"Great. That cheers me up a lot!" you say.

"First, you must know the power of the Golden Sword. The sword, you see, gives its owner the power to use it. Even if you have never held a sword before—"

"I haven't!" you interrupt.

"—the Golden Sword gives you the power to become an expert swordsman. This may help you or it may not!"

You get your chance to use the Golden Sword sooner than you'd imagined. Suddenly you find yourself tangled in the low, wiry branches of a tree. You attempt to pull away, then realize that the tree branches are *pulling you in!* Dry leaves choke you as you feel yourself being drawn in tighter and tighter.

"Use the sword! Use the sword!" your companion cries.

You hack at the branches with the Golden Sword. Can you free yourself?

Pick a number—any number.

If you picked an even number, turn to PAGE 24.

If you picked an odd number, turn to PAGE 26.

You made the wrong choice.

But don't feel bad.

You wouldn't have enjoyed Dragonwalk anyway.

No TV.

And you can't get a good hamburger anywhere.

The only ones who eat well in Dragonwalk are the dragons. But let's not bring that up. It's a really tasteless subject, don't you think? *Chomp, chomp, chomp, chomp, chomp!*

THE END

"Well, I guess I'd better just go ahead and not stop to think," you tell yourself. You raise the Golden Sword and rush toward the smallest dragon.

The little dragon (about as tall as a three-story building!!) roars its fury and bounds forward to meet your challenge. As your eyes grow wide in horror, the small dragon accidentally bumps into the middle dragon.

The middle dragon turns in anger and rises on its hind legs, swiping a claw furiously across the throat of the smallest dragon. The smallest dragon fights back, digging its teeth into the foreleg of the middle one. In a moment, the biggest dragon joins the fight. The ground shakes as the giant beasts slash and bite each other in a furious battle.

You cannot believe your good luck. They are fighting each other to the death while you stand and watch!

Too bad you were standing so close! Because when the biggest dragon lifted the middle dragon high in the air and then smashed him to the ground, you just happened to be standing on the spot where the middle one landed. (And since it was the middle one, it only weighed 6,000 pounds, give or take an ounce or two.)

Tsk, tsk. Such a fine beginning.

Such a flat ending.

THE END

24

You fight valiantly against the grasping branches of the evil tree. But the more branches you hack away, the faster new ones grow to take their place. You realize you cannot defeat the tree on your own. Its grasp is tightening. You struggle to breathe.

"Help me! Please—I need help!" you cry.

Do not give up hope. If you have chosen the right companion to accompany you, you may still have a chance.

Did you bring Bendux, the wealthy man, with you? If so, it's time to give up hope. His money is of no use against a tree. Ravenhurst has claimed another victim. Close the book. Take a rest. And then try your luck in Dragonwalk again.

Did you bring Elkar, the knight-warrior? If so, there is a 50-percent chance that he can free you by the strength of his sword. Flip a coin. If it's heads, turn to PAGE 30. It it's tails, turn to PAGE 32.

If you brought along Chalidor, the apprentice sorcerer, there is a 33-percent chance that he can conjure up a spell to defeat the tree. Pick a number from 1 to 9.

If you picked 1, 3, or 9, turn to PAGE 27.

If you picked 2, 4, or 6, turn to PAGE 34.

If you picked 5, 7, or 8, turn to PAGE 40.

The dragons line up to meet your challenge. The Golden Sword is heavy in your hand as you attack the smallest one first.

Who is that screaming so loudly as you plunge the sword forward? It is *you!* Fear, the challenge to succeed, and your hope of freeing Dragonwalk of its captors drive you forward. Again and again you thrust the blade toward your target.

The smallest dragon (only about three stories tall) rears back its head and prepares to strike—but you strike faster!

You attack the legs, move up to the knees, dodge and dart out of the way of its fierce, hot breath. The other dragons roar their disapproval as the smallest dragon drops to its knees, then falls defeated on its side.

Victory!

But a short one. The largest dragon is set to avenge the death of his companion. The ground trembles beneath his angry footsteps. The air turns hot and wet.

"No knight has ever gotten this far before!" Merle yells from behind a bush.

"What?" You turn to try to hear what he's saying over the roar of the dragon, and you accidentally drop the Golden Sword! The largest dragon sees an advantage and makes a dive toward you. Can you pick up the sword in time?

Turn to PAGE 28. Fast!!

You grasp the Golden Sword tightly in your hand, your heart pounding as the tree limbs tighten themselves around you. "I— I can't breathe!" you cry.

You swing the sword wildly, slashing out at your captor. Slash again. And again. The Golden Sword cuts through a grasping limb, tears the bark off another. You begin to swing more frantically, faster and faster, cutting and slashing, and the limbs begin to fall to the ground.

You are winning. The tree seems to be loosening its hold. The Golden Sword is slashing your way to freedom.

Then suddenly, the massive trunk begins to part. The tree draws open like a giant cave, and you feel yourself being sucked inside.

Now you are in darkness. You are inside the tree, trapped in a black, hollow cave, still waving the Golden Sword, although there are no longer limbs to attack.

Are you a permanent prisoner of this silent foe? Or can you defeat the tree from the inside?

Raise the Golden Sword. Keep hacking at the trunk—and turn to PAGE 46.

"I've never seen anything like this tree," Chalidor says.

"I haven't, either," you cry. "But I wish you'd stop admiring it and do something to get me out of here!"

"No sooner said than done," Chalidor says, but his voice doesn't sound confident. "I know a good spell of disappearance. It never fails."

Chalidor begins waving his hands in the air and chanting at the top of his lungs. Stacy watches eagerly as the sorcerer begins to whirl and sway as he chants. The tree leaves choke you and the branches grow even tighter.

Will the spell of disappearance work?

Well . . . yes and no.

Chalidor claps his hands twice. There is a puff of red smoke.

"He's gone!" Stacy cries. "Chalidor disappeared!"

And with him, your hopes are gone, too. Better luck next time!

THE END

The dragon dives—and misses. The heat of his breath burns the edges of your clothing black. "Don't most knights carry shields?" you ask yourself.

But you have little time to think of equipment. The giant dragon is rising up from the ground, arching its serpentine neck, preparing to strike again.

You make a grab at the Golden Sword. You miss. It seems to be wedged under a stone. You pull at it. The dragon strikes. You throw yourself out of its path and roll away from its gnashing teeth.

You pull at the sword with all your strength. You've freed it. It gives you new courage.

Again and again you slash at the dragon's legs, sometimes hitting nothing but air, sometimes hitting your target. Soon the blows of the Golden Sword have an effect on your terrifying foe. The dragon slows down as you hack away at it, its energy flowing out from a dozen tiny wounds.

Encouraged, you renew your attack.

The giant dragon's face fills with surprise. But no one is more surprised than you as it lurches forward and falls onto its face, silent and dead.

Only the middle dragon remains. You do not pause to take a breath. You turn to face this medieval monster.

Go on to PAGE 29.

But the look in the dragon's eyes is not one of anger, but of grief. With its two companions gone, the middle dragon has lost all its fight. It offers no resistance as you plunge the Golden Sword through its heart.

You are victorious, and because of you, all of the people of Dragonwalk are victorious. The sorcerer Merle rushes out to thank and congratulate you, followed by Stacy, who is still shaking her head in disbelief, followed by the grateful peasants and townspeople of Dragonwalk.

"Many knights have failed, but you have succeeded," Merle says. "It is in my power to reward you with one wish. Wish for anything in the kingdom, and it is yours."

"Wow!" you tell yourself. "Anything in the kingdom. Gold! Diamonds! Wealth! What shall I ask for?"

"I wish we were back in Grandma Carmen's house," Stacy says suddenly before you can get out your wish!

Pop!! The two of you are back in the attic of Grandma Carmen's house. The sorcerer has sent you back just a little bit in time. You have just discovered a secret passageway. You know you want to go through it and explore—but Stacy doesn't want to go. You do not remember anything that has happened to you in Dragonwalk. What will your next adventures be like?

Turn to PAGE 6.

"The Sword of Elkar has never failed!" Elkar screams, drawing his blade. His sword clangs against the tightening branches of the foul tree. Slash and tear. Slash and tear. The branches fall, and the ground becomes sticky with a blood-red sap. Slash and tear. Slash and tear. The Sword of Elkar works its power.

In a few minutes, you are freed. You fall to the ground, half-crawling, half-rolling out of the grasp of the tree. You turn to Elkar and say, "Thank you." It isn't really enough, but you don't know what else to say.

"Perhaps later I will be thanking you," he says, wiping the sap off his sword with dry leaves.

"Wow! That was exciting!" Stacy cries. "I'm starting to like it here!"

"Was that Ravenhurst?" you ask, taking a few practice swings with the Golden Sword.

"We have many miles to travel and many foes to conquer before we meet Ravenhurst himself," Elkar says grimly. "Now before we journey on, we must rest. It wouldn't be wise to travel in this forest while tired."

Go on to PAGE 31.

The three of you take a short nap in the shelter of the trees. Your close call has exhausted you, and you fall asleep immediately and sleep soundly.

While you sleep, a small figure creeps out from behind a bush. It is an elf-thief, one of hundreds who prowl the forest, stealing to live. The elf-thief, dressed in forest green to blend into the surroundings, has his eye on Elkar's sword. What a price he could get for it!

Silently, the elf-thief darts across the forest floor. Elkar's gleaming sword is only a few yards from his grasp. If the elf-thief grabs the weapon and escapes with it, Elkar will surely be doomed. No one survives for long in this dark forest without a weapon.

Will the elf-thief be successful? There is a 40-percent chance that he will steal Elkar's sword.

Pick a number from 1 to 10.

If you picked 3 or 10, turn to PAGE 43.

If you picked 1, 4, 5, or 8, turn to PAGE 38.

If you picked 2, 6, 7, or 9, turn to PAGE 52.

"The Sword of Elkar has never failed!"
Elkar screams, drawing his blade. You cannot see anything, for the tree branches cover your face, scratching you and pressing you into the trunk of the foul tree. But you hear the *clang, clang* of Elkar's sword against the rotten wood of the branches.

Clang! Clang! Elkar hacks away at the branches that hold you prisoner.

And then you hear a scream, Elkar's scream. The sound of sword against tree branch has stopped. "The tree—it's got him, too!" Stacy screams, in a horror-filled voice that no longer sounds like a little girl's.

Elkar is a prisoner of the tree branches now. You are both doomed. The Sword of Elkar has failed for the first—and last—time!

"Someone's coming!" Stacy cries.

Is it possible you can still be rescued?

"I think it's Chalidor, the apprentice sorcerer! Yes—it looks like him!" Stacy cries.

This is your last chance. There is a 25-percent chance that Chalidor will rescue you from the grasp of the tree.

Pick a number from 1 to 8.
If you picked 4 or 6, turn to PAGE 35.
If you picked 7 or 8, turn to PAGE 36.
If you picked 1 or 2, turn to PAGE 37.
If you picked 3 or 5, turn to PAGE 41.

"Do not worry. I will defeat the evil of this tree with a spell my grandfather taught me," Chalidor says.

"Hurry! Hurry!" Stacy cries.

Chalidor struggles to remember the spell. Finally, after what seems like hours, he recites a few words, sprays some kind of powder in the air, and waves his arms.

The spell works! You can feel the branches loosening, loosening—and then disappearing! In place of the tree that held you captive stands a tall knight, dressed in bright green armor and carrying a brilliant green sword and shield. "You have not escaped yet!" the knight growls, raising the green sword menacingly above his head.

"I knew that it was you, Zabbo!" screams Chalidor, backing away. "Zabbo, Knight of the Trees—prepare to face the Golden Sword of Dragonwalk! Let's see what your foul magic can do against *its* power!"

You have no choice but to fight this knight in green. You raise the Golden Sword. It seems to pull you forward, to pull you into the battle. The Golden Sword clangs against the green shield. Again. Again. You thrust forward, moving as if in a dream, fighting this experienced knight as an equal. For that is the power of the Golden Sword—it gives you the power to use it!

Do you defeat Zabbo, Knight of the Trees?

Turn to PAGE 42 to find out.

"Well, well—what have we here?" cries an unfamiliar voice.

"Hey—you're not Chalidor!" you hear Stacy cry. "Who are you?"

"I'm the Tree Keeper," the voice says. "I'm just making my rounds, seeing if my trees trapped anything for my wolves' dinner! Wow! Look at that!"

You can't see the Tree Keeper's face because of the branches and leaves that cover you—but you can imagine that he's smiling!

THE END

"Stacy—is it—is it really Chalidor?" you manage to cry out as the leaves tighten around your face.

Silence.

"Stacy?"

"I'm sorry," she says quietly. "I didn't really see anyone coming. I just thought it might cheer you up."

Wasn't that nice of Stacy?

Too bad you can't thank her properly—but you're a little wrapped up in other matters!

THE END

"It is I—Chalidor!" a familiar voice cries.

"Help them! Help them!" Stacy screams.

The apprentice sorcerer goes to work, casting a spell to free you and Elkar from the trees that imprison you. "Hmm .... let's see ... what is the proper incantation? Um .... forsooth! I can't seem to remember the words! I don't suppose there's time for me to go home and look them up, is there?"

"Please! Please!" Stacy cries.

The sorcerer mutters some words. Then he mutters some other words. "Hey—look!" he cries. "I've done it! I've made it rain!"

Sure enough, rain begins to batter the trees and forest ground. "I've never been able to do that before!" Chalidor cries proudly.

Needless to say, you are not impressed.

Needless to say, you also have no need of an umbrella.

Needless to say, you are also in no position to read any further.

THE END

A wide grin breaks out on the elf-thief's face as he wraps his small hand around the handle of Elkar's sword. But his smile turns to open-mouthed horror as Elkar reaches forward and grabs the intruder by one leg.

"NO!" screams the elf-thief in terror.

"What have we here?" Elkar asks, tightening his grip. "Aha. A forest insect, I see. I shall smite it with my bare hand."

"Spare my life! Spare my life, and I will reward you!" the elf-thief begs.

The noise awakens you and Stacy. "What a cute little man!" she cries.

"Cute?" cries Elkar. "He would cut our throats for a hen's egg." Elkar grabs the elf-thief around the waist and begins to strangle him bare-handed.

"Wait!" you cry. "What did he say about a reward?"

The elf speaks: "Spare my life, kind knight, and I will give you this potion stolen from Ravenhurst's own cabinet. If slipped into Ravenhurst's drink, this potion will cause him to turn silly. Ravenhurst knows of its danger and has kept it locked up. Take it, please, in return for my life."

Do you choose to spare the thief's life in exchange for the potion? If so, turn to PAGE 50.

If you think it better not to trust the thief, allow Elkar to strangle him, and then turn to PAGE 44.

"I will free you from this tree!" Chalidor cries.

"Hurry! Hurry!" Stacy screams. "The tree—it's—it's—"

"Quiet!" the young sorcerer commands. "This is a simple spell, but it requires concentration."

Chalidor throws a white powder into the air and begins to chant in a peculiar language you've never heard. Then he throws some more powder in the air, closes his eyes tightly, and chants some more.

A few seconds later, you are free of the tree. Chalidor has kept his promise.

You raise your wings and soar up toward the sky, away, away from the grasping branches that held you prisoner. You raise your tail feathers to catch a wind current, hold out your wings, and float high above Stacy and the startled sorcerer.

"Hmmmmm," you say to yourself, opening and closing your beak, "a tasty earthworm would sure hit the spot right now."

You swoop through the sky, free as a bird—which you are, thanks to Chalidor's spell.

And, thanks to Chalidor's spell, you are free of the tree—and as far as rescuing Dragonwalk goes, you are free of any hopes—and you have reached

THE END

"It is! It's Chalidor!" Stacy cries. "Quick—can you help us?"

Chalidor takes a small, tattered book from his robe. "Hmmm . . . tree spells . . . tree spells. I don't know. I've never—I—I'm just an apprentice, you know." He searches desperately through the little book as you feel yourself unable to breathe under the tightening tendrils of the tree.

Then suddenly the tree branches seem to melt away. You are free. Elkar is also free. You are staring at dark brown puddles on the forest floor. Chalidor has cast a spell that melted the trees instantaneously.

"I don't believe it! It worked!" Chalidor cries. "I have rescued you!"

"And I have failed," Elkar says grimly. "The Sword of Elkar has seen failure." He turns away, embarrassed. Then he turns back to you. "Perhaps you would like to change traveling companions now," he says quietly. "Perhaps you would rather journey on with the sorcerer than with me."

You must choose again. Which of these men will you take along with you?

Make your decision. Then turn to your next adventure on PAGE 44.

"Your sword could not cut through my branches," Zabbo yells, his green sword swiping the air in front of your face. "What makes you think you can defeat me in my human form?"

You do not answer. You allow the Golden Sword to do the talking. It sings as it cuts the air, cuts through his defenses. A powerful swing of your arm, and the Knight of the Trees loses his shield.

He's backing away from you now, backing away from the power that guides the Golden Sword. Stacy and Chalidor look on from the trees as you swing and swing again.

You cut through the armor.

"I am hit," Zabbo cries. But he fights on. Sword clangs against sword in the dark forest—until your power overwhelms him. He sinks to one knee.

"Finish him! Finish him—or he will sprout up again, as he has many times!" Chalidor warns.

You drive the Golden Sword forward and deliver the final blow.

You sink to your knees. You are exhausted.

"No time to rest!" Chalidor cries, pulling you to your feet. "Ravenhurst will soon know that he has lost his forest knight. We must go forward. We must leave this forest!"

More adventure awaits on PAGE 44.

Silently, the elf-thief creeps up to where the three of you sleep. He wraps his little hands around the hilt of Elkar's sword and pulls the sword from its scabbard.

Then suddenly he stops.

"The Golden Sword of Dragonwalk!" he tells himself, his gray eyes growing wide.

Will he put down Elkar's sword and take yours instead? You sleep soundly, unaware that the small creature is staring at you and your sword with popping eyes.

After a few seconds, he turns and runs. He doesn't look back. He disappears into the forest.

Did your sword frighten him away? Did the power of the legendary weapon cause him to forget his thievery?

Or did he run to tell someone else—someone more powerful—about you and the Golden Sword?

You continue to sleep under the dark trees, unaware of these or any other questions.

Wake up now. You don't want to sleep for too long in this evil place. Wake up— and turn to PAGE 44.

"Hey—where'd Stacy go?" you cry, looking around and not seeing her. "Stacy! Don't wander off!"

"I'm over here!" you hear her call, from about fifty yards away. "Look at the big bird! Wow!"

Big bird?

You and your companion race toward Stacy's voice. You see her standing in a small clearing. "Stacy, what are you talking about?" you yell angrily. You are exhausted and don't want Stacy to get you into any new adventures if it can be helped.

"I've never seen a crow this big," Stacy says, pointing to a giant black bird about the size of a station wagon.

"That's not a crow! That's a carrier buzzard!" your companion screams. "We've got to get away before it—"

He doesn't get to finish his sentence. There is no time to get away. Before you realize what is happening, the giant black bird has swooped under you, grabbed you up in a giant talon, and hoisted you onto its hot, feathery back.

"Run, Stacy—run!" you yell. But she cannot escape, either. And in a few moments she is plucked off her feet and dropped beside you on the bird's back.

Go on to PAGE 45.

Your traveling companion struggles, but he, too, is taken captive and forced aboard the fast-moving bird. The bird flaps its black wings and prepares to fly. You hold on to its neck, fear keeping you from attempting escape.

With great effort, the bird lunges up toward the sky. You can feel the wind rush past as you struggle to keep your balance on the flying bird.

"We've been kidnapped. I don't know by whom," your companion says. "But our weight is keeping this bird from climbing very high in the sky. The forest ground is soft beneath us. I think we can jump off safely from this altitude."

Jump? Jump off a bird that's high in the sky? The idea doesn't exactly appeal to you. But you realize that it may be safer to jump off and try to escape than face what awaits you when the bird reaches its destination.

The three of you have a 50-percent chance of surviving a jump off the carrier buzzard. Good luck!

Pick a number between 1 and 100.

If you picked an even number, turn to PAGE 48.

If you picked an odd number, turn to PAGE 57.

46

Fear drives the Golden Sword hard into the tree trunk. Fear drives your arm forward again and again. The *clang* of the sword echoes in your ears as you batter the walls that hold you prisoner.

Daylight.

You have broken through.

You gasp at the fresh air, the sweet fragrances of the forest invading the tree trunk. The tree seems to give up. You push your way out of the trunk. The tree withers and dies at your feet. The ground is drenched in sticky, green sap.

Go on to PAGE 47.

"I made it! I'm free!" you call out, holding the Golden Sword high above your head.

But there is no one to hear your cheers.

"Stacy? Stacy?" you cry. You look desperately for her and your new companion.

Gone.

Only distant birds answer your worried calls. Stacy and your companion must have been kidnapped while you battled inside the tree.

You must go after them! You must find them! But how shall you go? Should you hurry through the tangled forest, hoping to avoid such traps as the grasping tree, or keep following the path you had begun?

A wide river cuts through the forest and runs in the same direction as the path you were taking. Should you avoid the perils of the forest and brave the unknown dangers of the river? Traveling on the water would certainly be faster. But where would it lead you?

It's your decision. If you choose to continue through the forest in your search for Stacy and your new companion, turn to PAGE 54.

If you wish to take your chances on the fast-flowing river, turn to PAGE 51.

48

The wind rushes past your face. The bird swoops low, then up again, its wings straining under the weight of its heavy cargo.

How will you ever jump off? The bird's feathers are hot and sticky. You feel as if you have been glued onto its back.

"Jump! You must jump!" your companion screams.

You grab Stacy and hold her tightly. You close your eyes and lean to the side. You lean farther and farther until—you've done it! You've fallen off! You're falling!

You and Stacy are both screaming. To the right you can see your companion falling through the sky a little above you.

Will you land safely on the ground?

No.

The crafty carrier buzzard is not about to let you escape. The bird efficiently flies under you, catches you on its back, then swoops to retrieve your companion.

You are right back where you started. The bird turns in the sky toward whatever evil awaits you.

And too soon the bird brings you to its destination, a small village of mud huts, crowded and filthy, with ragged goats and scrawny, pale chickens walking or standing in the dirt roads between the huts. Several strange-looking people appear as you land.

Go on to PAGE 49.

They are dressed in blue capes; their faces and hands are painted blue. They walk bent over, leaning forward on jagged walking sticks. Their eyes are wild and their mouths are arched in insane, toothy grins.

"Witches!" your companion screams. "What do you want with us?"

The witches use their walking sticks to pin you to the ground.

"Our business is with Ravenhurst—not with you!" your companion screams.

"Our business is with Ravenhurst, too," says one of the blue-faced witches in a shrill, high-pitched voice. "What a ransom he will pay for you! How grateful he will be to us when we hand you over to him in neat bundles, ready to be tortured and killed! Ha ha!"

"We've got to get out of here!" you tell your companion. "I still have the Golden Sword. Can we escape from these people?"

The answer to that question is *maybe*. It all depends upon whom you have chosen as a companion. The right companion can get you out of this mess. The wrong companion—well . . . let's not think about it!

If your companion is Elkar, the warrior, turn to PAGE 56.

If your companion is Chalidor, the sorcerer, turn to PAGE 62.

If your companion is Bendux, the man of wealth, turn to PAGE 63.

BOOOOOM!!

That was the sound of the jug containing the elf-thief's potion exploding a few minutes after you spared his life.

The entire forest shook from the blast.

There's a valuable lesson to be learned from this: Never trust an elf-thief.

Too bad you'll never get to apply this lesson in later life, since you don't get a later life in this adventure.

But don't go to pieces. Pull yourself together and try another journey through the dangers of Dragonwalk.

THE END

You walk down to the edge of the dark gray waters. You begin to pace by the water, trying to figure out how to make a boat that will carry you downstream.

"I don't know where I'm going, but I've got to get there as fast as I can," you tell yourself. Of course it doesn't make any sense—but what *does* in this land of evil?

"Footprints!" you cry. Sure enough, on the wet bank are the footprints of at least four or five people—recent footprints. "I've made the right decision," you tell yourself.

Suddenly your thoughts are interrupted by a rude croaking sound down by your ankles. "Help me, sir," a voice croaks.

You look down to discover a large, brown frog hopping gently at your feet. Fearing another trap, you raise the Golden Sword high, ready to strike.

"I can help you. Please, sir—I can help," the frog croaks, hopping up and down more vigorously. "I can help you find your friends. Ravenhurst has cast this spell on me. Touch my head and you will break the spell. Free me, sir, and I will help you."

Is it a trick? Does the frog know where the kidnappers took your companions?

If you think the frog is telling the truth, touch its head and turn to PAGE 58.

If you think this is another of Ravenhurst's tricks, try to catch the frog—and turn to PAGE 60.

A wide grin breaks out on the elf-thief's face as he grabs the handle of Elkar's sword. Slowly, silently, he pulls it from its scabbard. The sword is in his little hands now, and he scampers happily away with it, back into the forest from where he came.

When Elkar awakes, he realizes immediately that his weapon is gone. "Elkar, what will you do?" you ask, afraid that he will abandon you now that he is defenseless against the horrors of the forest.

"I will retrieve my sword," he says calmly. He doesn't seem upset at all by the loss.

"But how will you find the thief? You cannot track anyone in this forest," you say.

"There is no need," Elkar says quietly. "Follow me."

He walks off into the trees, and you and Stacy follow close behind. He seems to know exactly where he is going. A few moments later, you see the sword. It is lying on top of a small elf dressed in green—the thief. The elf is struggling to climb out from under the sword, but he cannot escape. "What has happened?" the elf cries.

"The Sword of Elkar will not travel without me," Elkar explains. "That is its power. It cannot be stolen."

Elkar picks the sword up easily, and the elf-thief scampers to his feet. "What are you going to do—slay me?"

Go on to PAGE 53.

"I would not tarnish my sword with you," Elkar says. He kicks the elf-thief, a mighty kick that sends the small creature flying through the trees.

"Whew! Now maybe we can take it easy for a while," you say, giving Stacy an encouraging smile.

"I don't know what that means," Elkar says. "We are never far from danger in the forest of Dragonwalk."

Turn to PAGE 44 to see if Elkar is right.

"I'm not taking my chances on the water," you tell yourself. "Somehow I just feel safer on dry land."

You head back into the thick forest. Footprints! Could those be Stacy's and your companion's? They follow a narrow, dirt path through the bent and tangled bushes. You follow the path, picking up speed, running over the prints, running to find your lost friends.

A narrow beam of sunlight cuts through the trees overhead, forming what appears to be a spotlight on the grassy ground. And standing before you in that spotlight is a red object, a bright scarlet object that seems to be moving.

"What can that be?" you ask yourself, slowing your pace just a little.

As you approach you see that it is some kind of lizard—a scarlet lizard, preening in the sun.

You come nearer. You feel yourself drawn to it. You cannot resist it. It arches its neck and seems to grin up at the sun. You reach your arm forward. Something wants you to touch it. You must touch that scarlet lizard.

Your hand makes contact. You touch it. "*Owww!*" The red heat of its body burns your hand. The small lizard begins to grow.

You realize you've made a serious mistake.

How serious? Turn to PAGE 61.

Elkar is a mighty warrior, but he really should be sent back to warrior school for thinking he could defeat the entire coven of witches with his swordsmanship and yours. It seems as if you picked the wrong companion for this adventure.

He makes a nice-looking toad, though. Those witches really know their toad spells, don't they? And you and Stacy look terrific with those blue faces. They match your new capes so nicely.

Well, at least you got a new wardrobe and a whole new look out of this adventure. Just the same, it's probably best that this particular chapter comes to

THE END

You know, you really should look before you leap. That bird was flying a lot higher than you thought it was.

Yuccccccch. You've really made a mess of things—mainly of yourself.

It's really very inconsiderate of you to mess up this book like that. Let's hope you pull yourself together for your other adventures in Dragonwalk!

THE END

You reach down and timidly tap the frog on top of its head. The frog face begins to grow larger, and the frog body grows tall and takes human shape. Standing before you is a knight in green armor with the face of a frog!

"Prepare to die, fool!" he croaks, brandishing a long, green sword. "Do you not know that all forest frogs are soldiers of Ravenhurst?"

Go on to PAGE 59.

You have no time to answer, for the frog knight attacks quickly and with great skill. His green sword clangs against your golden sword as he presses you toward the water. It is all you can do to fend off his powerful thrusts, and you find yourself backing up, backing up—your feet are in the water— and still he comes at you.

"Hold on! We're coming to help you!" a voice calls from down the river bank as you struggle to keep from backing up any further. It's Stacy and your new companion!

"I thought you were kidnapped!" you cry, ducking under a vicious swipe of the green sword.

"We were looking for you," your companion cries. "Hollow trees often have tunnels that lead to exits in the forest. We were searching the forest for you!"

Clash! Clash! You swing the sword and take a step forward. You are back on dry land now.

"I'm coming to help!" your companion cries.

You are starting to win. Do you want the help? Or would you prefer that your companion stay and protect Stacy?

If you would like your companion to help you defeat the frog knight, turn to PAGES 64 and 65.

If you think you can handle the green swordsman without help, turn to PAGE 66.

60

You reach for the frog and catch it with your right hand. But suddenly the frog vanishes completely from your grasp. And as the frog disappears, Stacy and your companion reappear beside you.

"You—you're both okay!" you cry in amazement.

"We were here all along," Stacy says. "That frog cast some kind of invisible spell on us."

"It was no frog. It was a creation of Ravenhurst's," your companion says quietly. "You were wise to ignore its pleas. But now Ravenhurst will be angrier than ever. We must flee this place."

"Look—is that a boat down there by the river bank?" you ask, pointing to a dark object partly hidden by reeds.

"Let's go see!" Stacy cries.

Is it a boat? Turn to PAGE 68.

The scarlet lizard grows and grows.

It is taller than you now, and still it grows.

Why don't you run from it? Why are you frozen there, staring at it, watching it grow redder as it grows bigger and hotter?

Why can't you run?

Perhaps if you close your eyes, its scarlet spell will be broken, its hold on you loosened. Perhaps.

Do you choose to run? Or do you feel you must face this giant, red beast-creature?

If you choose to run, close your eyes tightly and sneak a peek at PAGE 67.

If you feel you must stay and face it— no matter what the consequences—turn to PAGE 71.

"I'll get us out of this with a special, powerful escape spell I've been practicing," Chalidor says. "Witches aren't the only ones who cast spells, you know."

"Hurry! Hurry!" you and Stacy both cry.

Chalidor mumbles some strange phrases over and over. And in a few seconds—poof—his spell of escape has worked!

Unfortunately, it has worked only for Chalidor and Stacy! You are still there, pinned to the ground, surrounded by blue-faced witches! "How could he do this to me?" you ask yourself.

You grab the Golden Sword, ready to begin what may be your last battle. But to your surprise, the witches leap back in terror. "The Golden Sword!" one of them cries. "Do not gaze at it, or we will all perish!"

They turn and run, leaving you alone in the village. "Now I've got to find Stacy and Chalidor," you tell yourself, still amazed at how easy your escape was.

You turn and head in the opposite direction of the terrified witches. You follow a narrow path deep into a thick forest. You don't know where you are or where you're going. You look for any kind of clue that will help you to find them.

The path disappears, then reappears at a wide river. A canoe rests on the bank. Should you try your chances on the river?

Turn to PAGE 54.

"Well," says Bendux brightly, "if ransom money is all you're interested in, that's no problem. I can pay you as well as Ravenhurst might."

His money bags are attached to his belt. He shoves away a witch who is trying to tie his hands and holds up one of the heavy bags. "Here. I will pay handsomely for our release. Take all my money and let us go."

To your surprise, the witches eagerly do as he says.

"My money has saved lives more than once," says Bendux, as the three of you walk quickly into the forest.

But he has spoken too soon. The witches quickly realize they have made a foolish mistake. They can keep Bendux's money—and hold you for ransom from Ravenhurst! You hear their footsteps as they hurry into the forest to recapture you.

"Run! Run!" you cry.

Can you outrun them—and their spells?

You have never run so fast, so blindly, so desperately in your life. Soon you realize that you have outrun them. But you have become separated from Stacy and Bendux. You make circles in the forest, but you cannot find them. Have they been captured?

You come to a wide river. A canoe rests on the bank. How will you find them? Should you take your chances on the river?

Turn to PAGE 54.

64

Can your traveling companion help you defeat the frog knight? It depends on whom you have chosen as a companion . . .

IF BENDUX, THE WEALTHY MAN, IS YOUR COMPANION, READ THIS:

"Here is a bag of gold!" Bendux cries to the frog knight. "Stop fighting!"

"A bag of gold?" croaks the knight. "Why didn't you say so in the first place?"

He puts down his green sword, hops over to Bendux, and greedily grabs the bag of gold. Then he turns toward you (you are still lying on the wet ground in pain), gives you a deep bow, and hops off into the forest.

"Ravenhurst's frog knights don't receive a salary," Bendux explains. "Their entire income consists of bribes. No one ever fights with them. Everyone just bribes them and they go away."

"I wish you'd told me that a few minutes ago," you say, getting slowly to your feet.

"I feel we are getting closer to Ravenhurst," Bendux says, changing the subject. "Look—is that a boat over there in those tall reeds?"

"Let's go see!" Stacy cries, eager to be away from this spot.

Is it a boat? Turn to PAGE 68.

IF CHALIDOR, THE APPRENTICE SOR-
CERER, IS YOUR COMPANION, READ
THIS:

The magic has run out for you. The frog
knight is already under Ravenhurst's spell.
No spell of Chalidor's is powerful enough
to interrupt Ravenhurst's spell.

In a few seconds, the frog knight has
touched you, Stacy, and Chalidor with his
green sword. The three of you are now little
green creatures who hop and croak. That's
right—you're frogs. (You catch on pretty
quickly for a member of a lower species!)

Too bad—but look on the bright side.
There are lots of big, juicy flies around the
river bank. And all that fighting has given
you a big appetite!

THE END

IF ELKAR, THE KNIGHT-WARRIOR, IS
YOUR COMPANION, READ THIS:

There is a 70-percent chance that Elkar
can win the battle against the frog knight.

Pick a number between 1 and 10.

If you picked 3, 6, or 9, turn to PAGE 69.

If you picked 1, 2, 4, or 5, turn to PAGE 70.

If you picked 7, 8, or 10, turn to PAGE 72.

"Stay back! Stay back!" you cry, driving the Golden Sword forward, pressing your attack. The frog knight continues to retreat, stepping back almost to the edge of the trees.

"I called you fool once," he cries, ducking under the arc of your sword, "and I call you fool again!"

With a hideous croak he bounds up into the air. Your sword swings under him, and as he lands, he swings his green sword down on you, knocking away the large piece of bark you had been using as a shield.

Again the frog takes a giant leap. This time, as he descends, he slams the handle of his sword into your shoulder. The pain rushes through your body. Your hand loosens its grip on the Golden Sword.

Again the frog knight leaps high into the air.

"Help!" you cry. "Please—I need help after all!"

The frog drives the sword handle down into your other shoulder. You cry out in pain as he prepares to leap again.

Is there still time for your companion to help you?

Quick—turn back to PAGE 64—and WATCH OUT! He's making another leap!!!

You close your eyes tightly.

The blinding scarlet color doesn't fade from your sight. It lingers under your eyelids.

You try to turn. You try to move.

You cannot.

The heat of the growing lizard holds you in place. You are a prisoner. You have no choice but to face this creature.

But when will it stop growing?

Open your eyes. And turn to PAGE 71.

Sure enough, it's some kind of strange-looking boat. Actually, it looks more like a rubber raft than a boat. And perhaps the oddest thing about it is the serpent face painted on the front of it.

"Let's get in it and go downriver," you say. "I just want to get away from here!"

Your companions reluctantly agree.

You climb in and lift Stacy in after you. Your companion mans the oars, and you begin to float downstream with the river current.

Suddenly, however, the boat changes direction. No matter how hard your companion rows, the boat moves in the opposite direction. "This boat has a mind of its own!" you cry.

A mind of its own—and a face! The painted face on the front pushes forward and begins to take shape. The eyes move, the mouth opens. You're not aboard a boat—you're aboard a living creature!

"Jump! Jump into the water! Quickly!" your companion yells. "Who knows where this creature is taking us!"

Do you stay aboard and find out? Or do you jump out and try to swim for shore?

If you choose to stay, turn to PAGE 74.
If you jump, turn to PAGE 85.

"The Sword of Elkar will ring true!" cries Elkar, running forward to join the battle. Unfortunately, falser words were never spoken.

In his rush to come to your aid, Elkar slips in the mud. As he falls, his outstretched sword hits a rock and the blade cracks off.

The frog knight easily runs Elkar through with his green blade, putting a sudden, violent end to the life of your traveling companion.

"Run! Let's run!" Stacy cries, seeing that the frog knight has been momentarily distracted by his easy victory over Elkar.

"Yes! Let's make a run for it!" you cry, following Stacy as she runs into the forest.

Will the frog knight catch up to you? Or will you escape so that you can continue your pursuit of Ravenhurst?

There is only a 50-percent chance that you can run away from the hopping foe.

Flip a coin. If it comes up heads, turn to PAGE 76.

If it comes up tails, turn to PAGE 78.

"The Sword of Elkar will ring true," Elkar cries, rushing forward to join the fight. And indeed, his sword does ring true. With one powerful thrust, he drives his blade deep into the frog knight's chest.

The frog knight's croak of horror fades as the knight begins to shrink. You stare in amazement—and relief—as the knight returns to the shape and size of a frog and hops slowly off into the underbrush.

"Let's get out of here!" Stacy cries. "This place gives me the creeps. Look—a boat!"

Is that really a boat Stacy has spotted in the tall reeds down the river bank?

Turn to PAGE 68 to find out.

The lizard is at least eight feet tall and still growing. And as it grows, its fiery color glows brighter until you feel as if you are staring into the sun.

The Golden Sword trembles in your hand as you struggle to lift it. You must defeat this devil-lizard before it attains its full height.

It takes every ounce of your strength to raise the Golden Sword, but you do it, and press it forward. The scarlet lizard's black eyes grow wide as your blade stabs at its chest.

The heat is almost unbearable, but you stab again and again.

The lizard's mouth opens wide in a snarl. Its black tongue lashes out at you. It is still growing, not ready for combat. You have gained a real advantage by striking early.

But even this advantage is outweighed by the size and heat of this monstrous lizard. You thrust the Golden Sword forward again and again, battling valiantly as the lizard continues to grow.

You are not aware that you have only a 50-percent chance of victory in this battle. It is all a matter of luck.

If today's date is even-numbered, turn to PAGE 73.

If today's date is odd-numbered, turn to PAGE 77.

"My sword will finish off this pesky frog," Elkar cries, joining the fight.

"Two against one is not the way of gentlemen," the frog knight croaks. He turns his head and begins to croak loudly, summoning help from other frog soldiers.

In a few seconds, you, Stacy, and Elkar are surrounded by croaking frogs. "We are outnumbered!" you cry.

"Just stay away from them! They cannot assume human shape unless you touch them!" Elkar cries.

The frogs hop toward you, eager to touch you so that they may grow and help their green friend. But you manage to leap away from them.

"Drive hard—drive fast!" Elkar commands his sword. He thrusts it forward and stabs the horrified frog knight through the heart. Immediately, the frog knight shrinks down to his earlier size. He hops away, followed by his fellow frog soldiers, who realize the fight has been lost and victory is yours.

"This victory brings us one step closer to meeting Ravenhurst himself," Elkar says, helping you up from the ground.

"Look—a boat! We can take it down the river!" Stacy cries.

Is that really a boat hidden in the tall reeds down the river bank?

Turn to PAGE 68 to find out.

The lizard has grown so hot, you feel as if you might melt. Yet the Golden Sword plunges forward again and again. It seems to be fighting on its own now. You struggle to stand up before this monstrous lizard, allowing the sword to control your arm, to fight the beast, draining your strength with each thrust.

An earth-shattering roar! The lizard is now ready to fight. Its black tongue darts toward you, slapping the ground, cracking like a whip. Giant yellow teeth are bared. The lizard snorts as it lowers its head and opens its mouth to swallow you.

And as it lowers its head, the Golden Sword takes a valiant swipe. Your arm swings in a wide arc. The blade cuts deep and true.

The red lizard's head flies into the air. It hits a tree and drops to the ground with a shattering crash.

You have killed it.

Its scarlet fades to gray. Its huge body stands upright, even though its head is no longer attached.

Suddenly, there is movement. You are sitting on the ground, trying to catch your breath. The headless lizard body begins to move.

Must you fight it again? What is happening?

Turn to PAGE 80.

"I have no control of this boat at all!" your companion cries, tossing down the oars in horror and disgust. "We are at the mercy of this thing—whatever it is!"

This "thing" continues to take shape as it carries you down the river. The serpentine head is now at the end of a long, gray neck. Arms and legs seem to sprout from the sides of the boat.

"A dragon!" Stacy cries. "We're riding on a dragon!"

But not for long.

Suddenly, the dragon walks onto the shore with you on its back. It dips its head low with a sudden jolt, and the three of you crash to the ground. The dragon stands above you menacingly, its teeth preparing for a tasty meal, its tongue darting eagerly at its black lips.

The dragon moves forward, then bends down to finish you off.

"No! No!" you cry. "It *can't* end this way!!"

And you're right.

Turn to PAGE 82.

There is an old expression in Dragon-walk. It is used every time an unfortunate baby is born in this dark kingdom. The doctor holds the baby up and says, "Better luck next time."

Sad to say, as the frog knight comes hopping up to you with his sword poised, this is an expression that also has to be said to you at this point in your travels:

"Better luck next time."

THE END

Again and again, the Golden Sword attacks. It seems only to annoy the scarlet lizard.

Suddenly the scarlet lizard rears back its head. The ground seems to shake and the red light grows so strong you cannot bear it. You raise your arm to shield your eyes.

And everything grows black. Black and wet.

"Hey—is that you?" a small voice cries.

It is Stacy's voice.

You open your eyes, but you cannot see anything in the darkness.

"Stacy—where are we?" you cry.

"We're inside the red lizard," she says in a trembling voice. "Eaten up. We're in its stomach, I guess."

"What?!" you cry, more in anger than surprise. "This is ridiculous! Inside a lizard's stomach?? Is this any way for an adventure to end?!"

Sad to say, the answer in this case is yes.

Does it make you feel any better to know that you gave the lizard a brief moment of indigestion?

THE END

"Run!" Stacy cries.

"Whaddaya *think* I'm doing?" you yell.

You turn back—just a quick glance. You see the frog knight hopping angrily at the edge of the trees. But he isn't coming after you!

"We made it! We made it!" you yell.

"Poor Elkar," Stacy says quietly, gasping for breath.

"Poor us," you say. Your victory celebration is short, for you realize that the two of you are now on your own in this evil forest. The Golden Sword weighs heavily in your hand. You are tired and hungry and—yes—very scared.

The forest grows dark. You cannot tell whether it is because of the thickening trees or the approach of evening. The two of you walk close together. There seems to be a natural path, which you follow although you don't know where it leads.

"We'll have to stop soon for the night," you say quietly.

"Out here?" Stacy asks, horrified.

"Well . . ." You start to say yes—but then you see something through the trees. "Look—a cabin!"

Go on to PAGE 79.

Without saying another word, the two of you make your way toward the cabin. Is it occupied? Does it contain friend or foe? You are too tired to care.

"I'm so tired," Stacy says, as you reach the cabin door. "I can't take another step."

Without thinking to knock, you push open the door and step inside. You walk into a large, bright kitchen.

"Where have you been?" Grandma Carmen asks angrily.

Silence.

You and Stacy are too shocked to speak.

"What are you doing here?!?" you ask.

"What? Why, I live here, of course!"

Sure enough, the kitchen looks very familiar. There you are—right back in Grandma Carmen's kitchen, right back in the world of today.

"But—but—you've ruined our whole adventure!" you blurt out.

"What are you talking about, child?" she asks, feeling your forehead to see if you have a temperature.

Don't try to explain, whatever you do. She'll never believe you. Just congratulate yourself for making it out alive. Take a breather. Enjoy some of Grandma Carmen's special pot roast. Then open the book again and try your luck once more against Ravenhurst and his evil sorcery.

THE END

Exhausted, you raise the Golden Sword and prepare to fight again. You drag yourself to your feet. staring at the headless lizard body, which is moving about.

"Oh, no! I don't believe it!" you cry as Stacy and your traveling companion climb out of the lizard's body.

"Well, it took you long enough to rescue us!" Stacy cries. "It was hot in there. I didn't like being swallowed."

"We owe you our thanks," your companion says.

"We owe the Golden Sword all the thanks," you say modestly, so pleased to see them again.

"Now we must flee deep into the forest," your companion says. "The red lizard was the pride of Ravenhurst's menagerie. When he discovers that you have killed his pet, he will come after us with a vengeance you cannot imagine."

"I'm too weary to go any further," you say. "I'm going to stay right here and face Ravenhurst once and for all. I'm tired of running. If our mission is to destroy Ravenhurst and rid Dragonwalk of his evil, I say let's stop running like rabbits and face his challenge!"

"Yay!" cries Stacy. She doesn't really understand what you're saying, but you say it so strongly, she feels she has to cheer.

Go on to PAGE 81.

"You're making a foolish mistake," your companion says. "This ground is Ravenhurst's. You do not dare fight him on his own property. You stand a much better chance on neutral forest ground."

This calls for one of the biggest decisions you will have to make. You are tired of running, tired of always being on the defensive. Do you stay and fight? Or do you go further into the forest where Ravenhurst cannot find you so easily?

If you wish to stay and fight, turn to PAGE 84.

If you think it best to listen to your companion's advice and go deeper into the forest, turn to PAGE 86.

The Golden Sword slipped out of your hand and bounced a few yards away when the dragon threw you off its back. Before you can retrieve it, the dragon bends its head low to take you into its mouth.

You fall back to the ground and kick it as hard as you can. The beast rears back in surprise and, in that instant, you grab the Golden Sword.

The giant head swoops down, angrily now, a roar from its throat shaking the forest trees. You time the thrust of the golden blade perfectly, catching the dragon just below the chin, slashing and cutting, using every ounce of strength you have.

Dark purple blood pours from the wound you have cut, pours over you and onto the ground, thick and hot. The roar of the dragon becomes a cry. *"You dare to attack Ravenhurst himself in his own land?!"* the dragon yells through its anger and pain.

You are battling Ravenhurst himself!!

The dragon begins to change shape. It becomes a falcon, its talons trying to tear off your head. But the Golden Sword stands firm against every attack.

The falcon becomes a leopard, the leopard a devil bat. But each incarnation seems weaker than the last, as the dark blood continues to stain the forest ground.

Go on to PAGE 83.

The final form the figure takes is human.
as the great sorcerer Ravenhurst — the Ravenhurst whose evil has enslaved Dragonwalk for so many years — lies dead at your
feet, slain by your courage and by the power
of the Golden Sword.

"We owe you a debt we can never repay,"
your companion says gratefully, still not
believing that Ravenhurst has met with
defeat.

"Now can we go home?" Stacy asks.

Surprisingly enough, the answer to that
question is yes! For standing right in front
of you is a very familiar passageway. The
passageway is wide open and very inviting.

You and Stacy run into it without looking
back. In seconds, you are back in Grandma
Carmen's house, back in that familiar attic
room, back in the safety of the present where
there are no dragons, no witches, no evil
sorcerers — until you dare to open up this
book again!

THE END

"Why are you always so stubborn?" Stacy asks, realizing that you plan to stay and fight right here. "Why can't you ever listen to good advice?"

Those are her last words.

You don't get any last words.

Ravenhurst has replaced his precious red lizard with three new red lizards, former humans.

Can you guess who they are?

"You do not dare fight Ravenhurst on his own property." That was probably the best advice you ever got. Too bad you didn't know it at the time.

But, cheer up. You look terrific in red!

THE END

You've jumped off the boat and into the river, but boy, do you wish you hadn't!

Ravenhurst has been up to his evil tricks here, as you may imagine, and he's raised the water temperature to a little above 220 degrees!

Isn't that enough to make you *boiling* mad?!?

Quick — climb back into the boat! That shade of red skin only looks good on lobsters!

All three of you — hurry — climb back into the boat — and turn to PAGE 74!

"Thank you for the good advice," you say. "Let's get going."

The three of you walk into the dark forest, making your way over thick brambles, hidden crevices, and deep banks of mud. More than one obstacle blocks your path. You are attacked by giant tarantulas, and the Golden Sword must go to work again, slashing and cutting until your path is clear.

Trees grab out at you. Stones beneath your feet turn into biting mouths that snap at your ankles. The flutter of bird wings becomes a roar as a pack of owls, their talons poised, plunge at you from tree limbs, screeching and crying as they attack. Once again, the Golden Sword strikes back at those who would block your path. The ground is soon littered with dying owls.

"This forest has vanquished all of Ravenhurst's foes in the past," your companion says, as you make your way wearily to a large, grassy clearing on a hillside. "But we have defeated the forest. We have survived its many threats."

"Good. Then we can go home," Stacy says, tugging at your sleeve, her eyes pleading.

"You have one more challenge," your companion says. "Ravenhurst himself. Having defeated his dark forest, you are ready to face the evil sorcerer himself."

Go on to PAGE 87.

"Will he find us here?" you ask.

"*You* have found *him*," your companion says. He points to a cave high on the hill. "The Cave of Dreams," he says quietly. "That is where Ravenhurst lives. If you can defeat him here, Dragonwalk will be forever freed of his evil."

You stare up at the black cave. A chill runs down your back. You can feel the evil in this place. The ground is damp, as if soaked with the blood of Ravenhurst's victims. The air is cold. The sky turns threatening.

How will you climb the hill to the Cave of Dreams? How will you find Ravenhurst and defeat him?

The answers to these questions depend entirely upon which traveling companion you selected long ago when you first entered Dragonwalk. Your fate is in his hands.

If you chose Elkar, turn to PAGE 92.
If you chose Bendux, turn to PAGE 88.
If you chose Chalidor, turn to PAGE 90.

"How do we climb up to the cave?" you ask Bendux.

But before he can answer, a tall figure appears at the mouth of the cave. The figure, dressed in a robe and cape of shimmering black, looms larger and larger as he floats down to the ground, the cape billowing behind him.

"How far you have traveled only to die," Ravenhurst says in a thunderous voice that echoes off the hill.

"You are mistaken, excellency," Bendux says, bowing his head. "We have traveled this far and made this treacherous journey to bring you gold." He begins to fumble in the large pockets of his robe, giving you a quick, meaningful glance as he does so.

Go on to PAGE 89.

You realize what Bendux is up to. By searching his robe for bags of gold, he is trying to distract Ravenhurst.

"Bring forth the gold and then die!" Ravenhurst bellows. "What is your delay, fool?"

Ravenhurst turns his back on you as he watches Bendux fumble in his pockets for the gold. It is your golden opportunity—your moment to use the Golden Sword. You raise it high and thrust forward with a powerful lunge.

Ravenhurst and his evil die at your hand.

"That was easier than I thought," Bendux says with a broad grin.

You and Stacy are laughing so hard, the tears are running down your faces — laughing from happiness and from knowing your mission is over. "Do you really have gold in your pockets?" Stacy asks Bendux.

"Of course not," Bendux says, grinning. "I would never carry cash — especially not in this neighborhood!"

You and Stacy begin to laugh again. You are still laughing when you find yourself back in Grandma Carmen's kitchen.

"What's so funny?" she asks.

How will you ever tell her?

THE END

"How do we climb the hill to find Ravenhurst?" you ask.

"There is no need," Chalidor says, his voice growing deep. "You have found him right here."

"What do you mean?" you ask, staring at the apprentice sorcerer.

Chalidor casts off the ragged robe he has worn the entire journey. Underneath he wears a shiny robe of royal purple. "I am Ravenhurst," he says, the evil glowing in his eyes. "I have been with you all along. I like to keep my foes in sight. It makes it so much easier to kill them."

"No, no — we trusted you!" Stacy cries.

"I am so sorry it has to end this way," Ravenhurst says, causing a jewel-handled sword to appear in his hand. "I was actually beginning to like you." He throws his head back and laughs a hideous laugh. His purple robe shimmers and shines as he moves. "I'll try to make your deaths quick."

"That's an amazing robe you're wearing," you say, your voice trembling, your hands shaking. "But there's something I should tell you. . . ."

"What's that?" Ravenhurst asks.

"You dropped something."

Ravenhurst bends down to see what he has dropped. As he does, you raise the Golden Sword and chop off his head.

Go on to PAGE 91.

You have done it. You have defeated Ravenhurst and his evil. Immediately, the sky brightens and the air turns warm. Birds begin to sing a sweet song in the swaying green trees.

A broad smile — a smile of relief and happiness — warms your face, and you see that Stacy is smiling, too. Your mission accomplished, you find yourself back in the attic room of Grandma Carmen's house.

You both have a lot to laugh about as you head down the stairs toward Grandma Carmen's kitchen and away from the world of Dragonwalk forever (or until you pick up this book again)!

THE END

"We will run up the hill with our swords drawn," Elkar says courageously. "We will fight Ravenhurst in his own lair, and together we will defeat him."

They are brave words, but they are only words. You wish you were anywhere but at the bottom of that hill. What hideous secrets are you about to discover in the Cave of Dreams? And what about Stacy? How could you drag her into this mess?

These are the questions you think about as you charge up the steep hill, sword raised, heart pounding. Before you realize it, you are at the mouth of the cave, the entrance to the mighty Ravenhurst's dwelling place.

"Now let's put these swords to work," Elkar says, taking a fighting stance. "Hey — where is my sword?"

Elkar's sword has vanished from his hand. Ravenhurst's magic has removed it. Weaponless, Elkar's courage drains. "Farewell," Elkar cries and dashes down the hill, defeated. You watch him as he runs. He never looks back once.

"Now what?" Stacy cries weakly.

"Forward. We have no choice," you decide. You run through the dark entranceway. Ravenhurst's magic doesn't seem to be able to take away the Golden Sword, for you hold it tightly in your hand.

Go on to PAGE 93.

Taking a deep breath, you burst into a lighted living chamber — and discover a white-haired little man, bent and shaking in a corner. "Who are you?" you cry.

"I — I am Ravenhurst," the little man squeaks in terror. "Pl-please, you don't have to sh-shout."

You take a few steps forward with the Golden Sword drawn. "What kind of trick is this?" you demand.

"You — you are not going to hurt me with that sword, are you?" the little old man stammers. "Pl-please p-put it down."

"You are Ravenhurst, who has held Dragonwalk as his domain?" you ask, growing braver by the second. "You are the mighty sorcerer?!"

Go on to PAGE 94.

"Well . . . I know a few tricks," the old man says, nearly fainting from fear. "How did you get up here? No one has ever gotten through the forest. You are the first to learn my secret — that I am a helpless old man."

"You have held this kingdom in fear," you accuse.

"I'll never do it again. I promise," Ravenhurst pleads.

"Hey — look at this blue vase," Stacy says from across the room. "It looks just like the one in Grandma Carmen's house." She picks it up. A passageway opens. On the other side, you can see the room in Grandma Carmen's house from which you came. "Come on — let's get out of here!" she cries.

"Do you promise to be good from now on?" you ask Ravenhurst, threatening him with the Golden Sword.

"Yes, yes, I promise," the old man squeaks.

Stacy is already running through the passageway, back to your grandmother's house. "I shall return if you do not keep your promise," you say boldly, and follow Stacy into the passageway.

As you reach your grandmother's house, you can faintly hear Ravenhurst calling, "Have a nice day" — the last words you ever hear from Dragonwalk, for this is

THE END